AMBER BROWN
SEES RED

Paula Danziger

AMBER BROWN SEES RED

Illustrated by Tony Ross

PUFFIN BOOKS
An Imprint of Penguin Group (USA)

PUFFIN BOOKS
Published by the Penguin Group
Penguin Group (USA) LLC
375 Hudson Street
New York, New York 10014

USA ★ Canada ★ UK ★ Ireland ★ Australia
New Zealand ★ India ★ South Africa ★ China

penguin.com
A Penguin Random House Company

First published in the United States of America by G. P. Putnam's Sons,
a division of Penguin Young Readers Group, 1997
Published by Puffin Books, a division of Penguin Young Readers Group, 2009

Text copyright © 1997 by Paula Danziger
Illustrations copyright © 1997 by Tony Ross

THE LIBRARY OF CONGRESS HAS CATALOGED THE G. P. PUTNAM'S SONS EDITION AS FOLLOWS:
Danziger, Paula, 1944–2004
Amber Brown sees red /
by Paula Danziger; illustrated by Tony Ross.
p. cm.
Summary: The year that she is in fourth grade is a difficult one for Amber,
as she tries to deal with escalating telephone fights between her divorced parents
and her father's impending return to take joint custody of her.
ISBN: 978-0-399-22901-5 (hc)
[1. Divorce—Fiction. 2. Schools—Fiction.] I. Ross, Tony, ill. II. Title.
PZ7.1.D2394Ao 1997 [Fic]—dc20 96-41227 CIP AC

Puffin Books ISBN 978-0-14-241261-9

Printed in the United States of America

19 20 18

To Bruce Coville

AMBER BROWN
SEES RED

Chapter One

I, Amber Brown, am going through a growth spurt.

Either that or the mirror's getting smaller.

I keep looking at myself from different angles.

Either my legs are getting longer or my pants are getting shorter.

Either my eyesight is getting bad or my bangs are covering my eyes.

I can practically feel myself getting taller . . .

My new shoes that I got only two months

ago at the beginning of fourth grade are too small.

I'm not sure that I'm ready for this growth spurt.

Sitting down on my bed, I pick up my favorite stuffed toy, the one that my dad won for me at the town fair.

"Gorilla," I say, "it's not that I'm complaining . . . . it's not that I want to stay the same size forever . . . . it's just that I would like something in my life to stay the same for a while."

The gorilla says nothing, but then he never talks. He just listens. At least that's one thing that stays the same.

I continue. "In the past two years, everything has changed. My parents separated. My father moved to Paris. My best friend, Justin, moved to Alabama. My parents divorced. My mom started dating Max. Then he asked her to marry him, and for us to

2

become a family. Now they're engaged. My favorite teacher, Mr. Cohen, stayed in the third grade, and I had to go into fourth grade. And now my feet are getting bigger. My legs are getting taller. Nothing fits the same way anymore.

"Say something," I tell the gorilla.

The hairy ape just sits there.

Looking around my room, I think about how my room is the only thing that hasn't changed. Doofy dancing-animal wallpaper, boring curtains and bedspread.

Even though the gorilla doesn't tell me, I know that I sound like such a complainer.

Things could be worse.

I know that.

I look at my mirror again and I see a spot on the right side of my face.

Things ARE getting worse.

I'm getting some weird disease.

I've already had chicken pox.

This must be vulture pox.

I touch the spot and it smears.

It's not vulture pox. (Which I'm not actually sure is a real disease.)

It's a mark from the pen that I used when I wrote a letter to my dad this morning.

Lately, he's been writing long letters about

how, even though he loves Paris, he's home-sick for me and for the United States.

"Amber Marie Brown. Get down here right now or you're going to be late for school," my mom calls up the steps.

Grabbing my knapsack, I rush downstairs.

It's Friday.

It's school.

It's math test day and I forgot to study.

Maybe I'll get lucky and something will happen so that the test gets canceled.

Chapter
Two

"Bulletin. Bulletin. Bulletin." Brandi runs up to me right after my mom drops me off at school.

"What is it this time?" I grin at her. "Did the janitor change another lightbulb? Did Mr. Cohen call Ms. Levine by her first name again? Has someone glued rhinestones on the school basketballs?"

"No." She stamps her foot. "That all happened last week . . . and I've already reported those things, so they're no longer bulletins."

"So what is it this time?" I continue to grin at my friend, who wants to be a tele-

vision reporter when she grows up and be-
lieves in being prepared for the future.

"Bulletin. Bulletin. Bulletin." She's jump-
ing up and down. "The school stinks."

"I thought you liked school. What's happened to make you think it stinks all of a
sudden?"

She holds her nose and giggles. "The
school stinks. It REALLY stinks. . . . Big
time! Really big time. I'm talking SKUNK
time. I'm talking SKUNK FAMILY time."

I start to laugh. "Skunks?!"

She nods. "Take a deep breath."

I can't. "I have a cold."

She tries to look serious. "It's a good thing
that I can give you this bulletin then. . . . We
may be sent home . . . the school really
stinks. . . . So, as Mr. Cohen said about ten
minutes ago, nose news is good news."

Now I start to laugh a lot. "Some schools
have snow days. . . . We may have a Skunk
Day."

Jimmy Russell and Bobby Clifford come running over to us.

They get down on their hands and knees, lift one leg, and pretend to be skunks.

I, Amber Brown, have always thought that they were little stinkers.

All of a sudden, there is the sound of whistles blowing.

The vice principal and the guidance counselor have gym whistles in their mouths.

Mr. Robinson, the principal, is using a megaphone. "Children. Go stand with your teachers."

I look for Mrs. Holt.

She's standing by the swings.

Brandi and I go over to her, moving closer to the school.

I still don't smell anything.

Mr. Robinson, the principal, is holding a megaphone.

Everyone is quiet as soon as he starts speaking.

That's because we all know that we'll get a very long detention if we're not quiet.

The announcement is made.

We have to go into the school and wait until arrangements are made to send us all home.

...... Until then we are to remain quiet, not cause any problems.

I see Mr. Cohen lean over to Ms. Levine and say, "That's using common scents."

Even though I like Mrs. Holt, my fourth grade teacher, I really miss having Mr. Cohen as my teacher. He's the best teacher in the whole world.

However, I, Amber Brown, am getting very curious about Mr. Cohen and his interest in the new kindergarten teacher. I was sort of hoping that he'd wait until I graduated from college to get interested in someone . . . . like me. Oh well, he'll probably be much too old for me by then anyway . . . . . . Probably ancient . . . . at least forty.

Oh well . . . Ms. Levine seems really nice.

"Line up by classes" is the announcement.

We do.

The next announcement is "Return to your classes."

We do.

Jimmy Russell and Bobby Clifford continue pretending to be skunks.

They get detention.

I personally think that Jimmy and Bobby are so used to having detention that they think it's a regular school subject . . . . . math, science, detention, English.

It's only October and already they have enough detentions to keep them after school until next February. By the end of this school year, I bet they'll have enough detentions to keep them after school until they graduate from high school.

Walking in, I can smell the skunks, even with my very bad cold.

It's gross, really gross . . . really, really, really gross.

Ms. Levine's kindergarteners are walking in front of us.

One of the little girls starts to cry, "I'm scared. I'm scared. I don't want to come in here. What if they try to get us? What if they bite us and give us rabies? What if they stink?"

Some of the other kindergarteners start to cry.

One of them wets his pants.

There's a little puddle around his shoe.

Something tells me that this is going to be a school day that I'm never going to forget.

Chapter
Three

Skunkorama.

Serious Skunkorama.

I, Amber Brown, don't think that there is a family of skunks.

I think that there is a skunk convention.

The good news is that I can smell again.

The bad news is that what I can smell is skunk.

Yuk. Yag. Double Yuk. Double Yag.

Mrs. Holt is covering her nose with her hand. "Class. Please take out your books for free reading time."

Saved. I'm saved . . . . no math test!

Hannah Burton raises her hand. "I thought we were going to have a math test. I studied."

The only smell worse than skunk is Hannah Burton.

Alicia Sanchez raises her hand.

"Yes." Mrs. Holt is still covering her nose.

"I don't feel well. This smell is . . ." Alicia barfs on her desk.

All of a sudden, I can feel my breakfast, Cheerios, milk, and bananas, working its way back up from my stomach.

Somehow I get my brain to push it back down again.

"Ewwwww." Hannah Burton makes a disgusted and disgusting face.

Personally, I think that Hannah Burton's face is normally disgusting.

Mrs. Holt hands Alicia some tissues. "You better go to the nurse. Naomi, go with her and then stop at the front office and ask them to send the janitor."

Barforama . . . Skunkorama . . . . This class is turning into Stinkorama.

Mrs. Holt drops some tissues over Alicia's barf so that we won't have to look at it.

I think I hear her mumble, "I should have called in sick today."

An announcement comes over the loud-speaker. "This is your principal speaking."

Mr. Robinson sounds like an airplane pilot.

"I just want to keep everyone informed of the situation. . . . Since this is Friday and we will have all weekend to try to eradicate the problem and get rid of the smell . . . we have decided to call off school for the day."

Our class starts to cheer, to whistle, to stomp their feet.

Even Mrs. Holt is applauding.

I can hear other classes making noise.

"Quiet!" Mr. Robinson screams into his microphone. "Quiet! Quiet! Quiet! Or we'll cancel plans to close the school."

It quickly quiets down and he continues.

"You will not be dismissed for a long time, though . . . so teachers will continue with classes . . . except for gym classes, which will be canceled . . . and, teachers, unless there is an absolute emergency, please send no more students to the nurse. Her room is filled . . . and no more janitor requests unless there is an emergency . . . he is very busy. Now to explain the procedure: We must personally contact each parent, guardian, or backup person on your records to let them know that you are to be picked up if possible or bused home, if someone is there to take charge. We also have to locate the bus drivers."

"We're going to be here all day." Jimmy Russell puts his head down on his desk.

"I can take care of myself," Vinnie Simmons says.

Yeah, right, I think. Vinnie is the kid who, in kindergarten, wanted to eat his chicken pox.

Mr. Robinson continues. "Since there are only two regular phones in the front office, we will also be using the fax machine phone . . . and several teachers will be using

17

their car phones and portable phones. It will take a while to reach all parents and guardians or backup people."

"'Backup people' sounds like singers who sing behind the stars," Roger Hart says.

"He means the name of the person who is to be contacted if your parents or guardians cannot be reached," Mrs. Holt explains.

"Maybe they also sing backup in a band," Bobby Clifford says.

I wonder whose name my mom put on my records as backup. It used to be my friend Justin's mother, but they've moved to Alabama.

I wonder what's going to happen to me.

This morning, my mom said that she was going to be at an important all-day seminar. My dad is so far away. My Aunt Pam is in California. I don't think that they will call them . . . and anyway, what are they going to be able to do?

I write a note to Brandi.

*Can I go to your house today?
My mom's at a business meeting*

She looks at the note and makes a face.
Writing a note, she passes it to me.

*I was just going to ask you
if I could go to your house.
My mom said she had a meeting
with someone somewhere. I
wasn't listening.... and my
dad's away on business. What
are we going to do? Do you
think we'll have to spend
all day here with the
skunks???????????*

After I read it, I look at Brandi and we
cross our eyes at each other.

Mr. Robinson says, "Now, teachers,
classes, proceed with your classwork until
further notice."

"Take out your books," Mrs. Holt says.

"What about the math test?" Hannah calls out.

"Shut up," the rest of the class tells her.

"Mrs. Holt. Tell them that they can't tell me to shut up," Hannah whines.

For a minute, it seems like Mrs. Holt is going to tell Hannah to shut up . . . but instead she just sighs and says, "Hannah, I'm the teacher in this room. I'll make the decisions. This is not a good time to test you. Now take out your books."

Tiffani Shroeder raises her hand. "Mrs. Holt, I'm worried."

"About what?" Mrs. Holt asks.

Tiffani, the vegetarian who belongs to animal rights groups, says, "Mr. Robinson says that they're going to eradicate the problem over the weekend. Does that mean that they are going to kill the skunks? That's not right."

Mrs. Holt sighs. "I don't know any more

21

than you do. Later you can ask Mr. Robinson about that. Take out your books."

Tiffani may be concerned about the skunks, but right now I'm worried about me.

I take out my book and wait to find out what's going to happen next.

Chapter Four

I, Amber Brown, wish that I hadn't drunk soooo much orange juice this morning.

I really wish I hadn't because I, Amber Brown, have to go.

It's a problem because we are no longer in our classrooms. We are sitting in buses in the school parking lot, and school buses don't have bathrooms on them.

There are kids on the bus from all grades, kindergarten through sixth.

I don't want to have to get up and tell one of the teachers, in front of everyone, that I have to go to the bathroom.

If I do, I'll die, just die, from embarrassment.

If I don't die, one of the teachers will have to escort me back into Skunk School and then when I get back on the bus, the sixth graders will yell out, "Hope everything came out all right."

It's all the skunks' fault.

The skunks have won.

They're still in the school.

So are Mr. Robinson, the principal, Mrs. Clarke, the vice principal, Mrs. Peters, the school secretary, and Mr. Jones, the custodian.

I, Amber Brown, could definitely make a joke about the animal skunks and the human skunks all still being in the school. But I won't. I actually like all of the people still in the school.

I also won't joke because that would be dangerous because I really don't want to laugh when I have to go this much.

I try to concentrate on other things.

I count the number of school buses.

There are a lot of them.

Some of the buses are the ones that normally bring kids to our school. Some are the ones that normally take kids to the middle school and the high school.

Buses filled with kids who have permission to go home will be leaving soon.

Buses filled with kids who are waiting for someone to pick them up are staying in the parking lot.

I am one of those kids who is waiting.

I am one of those kids who is getting worried about whether I am ever going to be picked up.

I am getting worried about holding it in until someone rescues me.

Trying to think of other things, I turn to Brandi, who is sitting next to me, and start singing, "One hundred smelly old skunks on the wall, one hundred smelly old skunks on the wall, take one down, pass it around .... ninety-nine smelly old skunks on the wall. ..."

Brandi joins in.

So do some of the other kids.

Jimmy changes the words. "Ninety-nine smelly old skunks on the wall, knock one down, kick it around ......"

Tiffani hits him on the head with her knapsack. "Skunk abuser."

Jimmy rubs the top of his head. "Ow!"

"Serves you right." Tiffani shrugs. "You can hurt people, just not animals."

Jimmy turns around and stares at her. "My father's got a name for people like you . . . . . 'tree huggers.'"

Tiffani folds her arms. "Sticks and stones may break my bones, but names can never hurt me."

"Skunk hugger." Jimmy sticks his tongue out at her.

"I may love skunks . . . but you smell like

one . . ." Tiffani sticks her tongue out at him.

"If you love skunks," Bobby grins, "you must love Jimmy if he smells like one."

Both Tiffani and Jimmy make gagging noises.

From the front of the bus, Mrs. Holt calls out, "Amber Brown. Brandi Colwin. Someone is here for you."

Brandi and I give each other high fives.

One of our mothers has finally gotten here.

We can get out of here, off the bus, to a bathroom.

Saved from a life of embarrassment . . . I look out of the bus, expecting to see my mom or Mrs. Colwin.

It's neither.

Chapter
Five

"Max. What are you doing here?" I look at my mother's boyfriend, actually my mother's fiancé . . . . my future stepfather. (But I try not to think of him that way. I like to think of him as just Max, this nice guy. If I think of him as "stepfather," then that means I've given up thinking that my mom and dad will ever get back together.)

He looks at me, pretending to be hurt . . . at least I think he's pretending. "Would you like me to leave? Would you like to go back on the bus?"

"No!" Brandi and I yell at the same time.

"You must be Brandi." Max smiles at her.

She smiles and nods.

He explains. "Amber, the school contacted your mom and then she called me to see if I could help by picking up you and Brandi. I changed my schedule. Your mom faxed signed permissions to the school . . . and, here I am."

It's weird.

I really like Max but it's sort of like he's totally becoming a part of our lives . . . . and like my father's almost not there . . . . like Max is becoming my father.

I think about my real father and I think about how he's almost becoming my unreal father.

It's hard to stay close to someone who I hardly ever see, who is basically just a voice. A lot of the really good times that my dad and I had seem so long ago.

Now it's Max who is there when we need him.

"Save us! Save us!" Kids on the bus yell out of the window. "Help! We're being held captive because of skunks!"

"Quiet down!" one of the teachers yells.

"Help! We are being held captive by skunks!"

I'm not positive but that sounded like Jimmy Russell.

"Detention!" the teacher yells.

With that detention added to all his others, Jimmy will have to come back from college for that punishment . . . . or maybe he won't even go to college. . . . It'll probably be a job or jail.

I remember an important fact.

I have to go to the bathroom.

"Wagons ho." I use the phrase that my Aunt Pam always says when she's ready to leave.

We go to the car.

Max pretends to be a chauffeur, opening the back door for Brandi and me.

We get in and drive off, leaving Skunk School behind.

"Pit stop!" I yell as we approach a gas station.

Max stops.

I run into the bathroom.

When I come out, Max and Brandi are pretending to be gas station attendants, washing car windows.

When I woke up this morning, I had no idea it was going to be like this.

Every school should have at least one Skunk Day a year, only without the skunks and without the smell.

I only hope that I can convince Max to take us to the mall.

Chapter Six

"You have one thousand, two hundred and eighty-two points." The arcade attendant tells us our total.

That's the most points I've ever gotten.

There are several reasons for all of those points.

One is that Max put a twenty-dollar bill into the token machine and the three of us played until all of the tokens were gone.

The other reason is that Max is really great on the bowling-ball machine and the basketball hoops. Brandi really scores on the

rock-and-roll machine and I am the champ
of the Skee-Ball machine.

The other is that we've put all our tickets together . . . . . . One thousand, two
hundred and eighty-two points.

Brandi and I look at all of the possible prizes.

There are so many.

Some need so many tickets.

I would really like the cassette-player juke-box, but it costs too many tickets.

Brandi and I keep looking at everything.

Max looks at his watch. "Come on, girls. Make your choices. It's time to go to the food court."

"In a minute, please," I beg.

Max doesn't seem to realize that these tickets are the closest thing that Brandi and I are going to have to paychecks for a lot of years. Allowances are different somehow and we're not old enough to baby-sit. So, our choices are important.

Should we get one big thing and share it? Brandi and I have done that before. We sort of share a mermaid doll that Max bought for me after I didn't win one in a burping contest.

Should we each get our own separate things?

"My stomach is starting to growl," Max says. "You girls have five minutes to make your choices and then we're going."

Max is beginning to sound like a father.

Brandi and I make our decisions.

We each get a small stuffed animal. She gets a dolphin. I get a monkey to go with Gorilla.

We also get some candy, two heart rings,

and three string friendship bracelets.

Brandi puts hers on.

I put mine on.

We give one to Max, who looks at it for a minute like he's not sure of what he's going to do with it.

He's got that look on his face that some grown-ups get just before they say, "Thank you. I'll put it away to wear sometime later," and then they never do wear it.

"Max," I say, "it's a friendship bracelet and

you put it on and never take it off. It's a friendship bracelet and it means a lot."

He thinks for a minute and then he puts it on his wrist and smiles.

The string just barely fits around his wrist.

We go to the food court.

Hamburgers.

French fries.

Soda.

It's a great Skunk Day.

While we're eating, Brandi goes, "Bulletin. Bulletin. Bulletin."

I put more salt on my fries. "Didn't you report the bulletin already today?"

"That was the skunk bulletin. This is one I forgot to mention because the other news was much bigger and much smellier." Brandi picks up the catsup bottle and pretends it's a microphone.

"Overheard in the front office. Starting next week, the new housing development is opening. Families will be moving in. New students will be arriving soon. And the teachers thought it would be a good idea for all of us to 'bond.' Mr. Turner, please explain to the listening audience what 'bond' means."

Brandi moves the catsup-bottle "microphone" in front of Max.

He talks into the "microphone." "'Bond' means to make contact, become close."

Brandi takes back control of the microphone. "And now, sports fans, here is the big news. The teachers said that they are thinking of starting a sports league to get everyone doing things together . . . . and the fall and winter sport will be . . . . ta da . . . BOWLING!"

Max and I look at each other and laugh.

We all go bowling, Mom, Max, and me.

I, Amber Brown, am one of the world's worst bowlers . . . but we have a good time.

Continuing, Brandi informs us, "And they're looking for coaches for the different teams."

Brandi looks at Max.

She knows we go bowling.

Max starts to look at his hamburger.

Brandi repeats, "They're looking for coaches. It's really only for Saturday afternoons."

"Please," I say, thinking about how much fun it would be to be on a team with Brandi and some of the new kids . . . once we meet them.

Max sighs and then smiles. "Sure. Instant family. Instant bowling team."

I think about what Max has just said. He and Mom aren't even married yet. He isn't even living with us . . . and already he thinks of us as family.

For a minute, I wonder where my father is . . . . what he's doing right now.

And then I think again about the team

and Max coaching it. "Bowling will be a ball."

Max groans.

Brandi throws a French fry at me.

And Skunk Day continues.

Chapter
Seven

"I think we're going to get married in April," my mom says. "And then we're going to Hawaii for our honeymoon."

"I've always wanted to go to Hawaii." I pass the broccoli to Max and then applaud.

My mom and Max look at each other.

"Honey. It's a honeymoon," my mom says. "Max and I will be going, just the two of us."

I, Amber Brown, am very disappointed. I have always wanted to do the hula and see a volcano.

"There's a good chance that the Danielses

will come to the wedding. If so, they may be staying in our house while Max and I are in Hawaii. Then you will be staying with them," my mother tells me.

The Danielses. Justin. My best friend from forever. My only best friend until he and his family moved to Alabama. (Then Brandi became my best friend who lives in New Jersey, where I live.)

When my mom and I went down to visit them, we only stayed for a weekend. Spring vacation . . . I'll get to see them for over a week. That's even better than hulas and volcanoes . . . although Justin's little brother, Danny, is a little like a volcano. By that time, the Danielses' baby will be born. It will be so much fun.

"If they can't come," my mom says, "Aunt Pam will either stay with you here or you will go back with her after the wedding and stay with her in California."

I'm really beginning to like this honey-moon.

"I have some questions." I look at Mom and Max.

Mom and Max look at each other and then look at me.

"Here goes," I say. "What do I call Max after you guys get married? What will my last name be? When is Max going to start living here? Am I going to always be an only child? Will we stay here? Will I still be going to Paris to see my dad this summer? Will I have to wear a dumb bridesmaid dress at the wedding?"

These are questions that I've been think-ing about a lot, ever since Max asked my mother to marry him and gave her a really pretty diamond and amethyst ring.

Every time I look at the ring, I remem-ber the diamond engagement ring and the gold wedding ring that my mom used to wear when she and my dad were married.

I look at Max and Mom and wait for answers.

Max starts first. "My name is Max. You've always called me that and that's what you can continue to call me. And you will still keep your last name, unless you want to change it."

I think about how upset my father would be if I changed my name. . . . At least I think he would be upset. Anyway, I love my name . . . . . Amber Brown. It's so colorful! If I changed it to Max's name, I would be Amber Turner. It would sound like I was a stone mover-arounder . . . Amber Turner.

My mom says, "After Max and I are married, we will live in this town. For the time being, we'll live in this house. As for your always being an only child, I'm not sure."

I, Amber Brown, like being an only child. It makes me very nervous just thinking about not being an only child.

She continues. "As for visiting your father this summer in Paris, that's already arranged."

"And the bridesmaid dress?" I bite my lip. "You're not going to make me wear some dumb frilly thing, are you?"

She shakes her head.

"Are you going to be wearing some dumb frilly thing?" I ask her.

"I did that once already and look where it got me." She shakes her head again.

I hate when she says something against being married to my dad. She hardly ever does that, but when she does, it really bothers me.

She puts her hand on mine and says, "I'm sorry I said that. It got me my wonderful daughter."

I smile at her.

She picks up some broccoli with a fork and tries to put it in my mouth.

I, Amber Brown, do not like broccoli. I

think that the only green stuff that people should eat is pistachio ice cream. My mother, however, does not agree.

"Neither of us will have to wear dumb frilly things to the wedding. I promise you, Amber." She puts some broccoli in my mouth when I open it to say "Thanks."

"I don't have to wear a dumb frilly thing to the wedding, do I?" Max teases.

My mom grins at him.

The phone rings.

"May I answer it?" I figure it's Brandi with a skunk bulletin.

My mom gives me permission and I rush into the living room to answer it. That way I can have some privacy for my call and they can have some privacy too.

I pick up the phone.

It's not Brandi.

It's my dad.

He asks me what I've been doing, how I've spent my day.

I tell him about the skunks but I don't tell him about Max.

He knows my mother's engaged because she wrote him a note, but I still don't want to tell him what a great day I've had with Max. Somehow it just doesn't seem right.

I listen to his news and then we hang up.

I stand there.

I am so excited . . . . so excited.

51

Then I get nervous.

Somehow, I don't think my mom is going to be as excited as I am.

But I've got to tell her.

I go back into the kitchen.

"Mom," I say. "Dad's moving back and when he does, he wants me to live with him part-time."

Chapter
Eight

My mom, Sarah Thompson, has gone totally ballistic.

I, Amber Brown, have never seen her like this.

Clearing the table, she's slamming dishes around.

The bowl of broccoli falls to the floor.

If I weren't so upset by the way my mom is acting, I would be celebrating the fact that there will be no broccoli leftovers.

A glass falls, breaks, and spills water all over the tablecloth.

My mom puts down the dishes, sort of crumbles into a chair, and starts to cry.

Max kneels down and puts his arms around her.

Putting her head on his shoulder, she sniffles and tries to stop crying.

I want to be hugging her, but Max is already doing that.

I don't understand why she's acting like this.

When my dad moved to Paris, my mom was mad at him. She said that he was running away from responsibility.

I heard that fight.

Dad had come over to the house to tell us that he was being transferred, that it wasn't his fault . . . that he would always support me financially and love me.

They yelled so much, I started to cry.

I start to cry now.

Max stops hugging my mom and comes over and hugs me.

It's the first time he's really hugged me like this.

I put my head on his shoulder, sniffle, and cry. My nose drips on his jacket.

My mother comes over and puts her arms around both of us . . . a group hug.

I sniffle again.

My mother sniffles again.

Her eye makeup has run all the way down her face.

I sit down.

"Amber," she says, "I'm sorry. I don't understand why I'm acting like this."

Actually, I, Amber Brown, am not sure I want to understand why she's acting like this . . . I just don't want her to be acting like this. It's so scary.

She continues sniffling and speaking. "It's just that everything is going so well. I love you. I love Max."

I think about how I love her . . . but I also love my father.

"I don't want to see things change, have to deal with HIM at holiday time, have to work out custody arrangements, have HIM back in my life."

HIM is my father, I think.

I am just so confused. I haven't spent a lot of time with my dad since he left, and I'm not even sure of how I feel about him. I just hate it that my mom is acting like this.

"I have to go upstairs," I say.

My mother takes a deep breath. "Honey. I'm sorry. It'll be OK."

"I have to go upstairs," I repeat.

"It'll be OK," she repeats.

I go upstairs.

First, I sit on my bed and cry for a few minutes.

Then I take out my "Dad Book," the scrapbook with pictures of my dad, the one that I talk to when I need to feel close to him.

"This is a mess, a real mess," I tell him. "Why didn't you talk to Mom first? Why don't you two just grow up?"

Skunk Day has turned into one of the longest days of my life.

It started out stinking . . . and it's ended that way.

Chapter Nine

"Bulletin. Bulletin. Bulletin. Bulletin. Bulletin." Brandi picks up a twig, pretending that it's a microphone. "Live . . . . from the playground . . . . it's Brandi Colwin."

"Five bulletins." I smack my forehead with my hand. "What a busy news day."

"This reporter is on the cutting edge of several late-breaking stories," Brandi tells us. "The first bulletin is about . . . . . . THE NEW STUDENT. He will be arriving in our class, 4-B . . . TODAY!"

"Is he cute?" Naomi wants to know.

"Does he know how to bowl?" Vinnie Simmons pretends to throw a ball down an imaginary alley.

"More news about that in the later edition." Brandi grins. "I've just told you all that I know at this time. Now for the second bulletin.

"The skunks were apprehended." She holds her nose.

Tiffani clutches her heart. "Oh no. Did they hurt them?"

Brandi shakes her head. "No. They caught them in a Havahart trap, one of those that don't hurt animals. Then they let them loose in a woods, somewhere far away."

Bobby snorts. "Yeah, right. If you believe that, I've got some land on Mars I'd like to sell to you."

"You are soooooooooo mean," Tiffani whines.

"Bulletin Number Three." Brandi holds up three fingers. "The skunks didn't just wander in. They were put there . . . . the alleged culprits have been identified."

"Who are they? How did they find them?" Alicia asks.

"Daniel Delaney. . . . You know, the one everyone calls Danny de Looney . . . . and his best friend, Marvin Allen."

Everyone looks at Fredrich Allen, who is in our class. "I can pick my nose but I didn't pick my brother."

"Ewwwwwww." Hannah Burton makes a face.

For once, I agree with Hannah Burton.

Brandi continues. "The teachers at the high school figured it out by how bad Daniel and Marvin smelled. The principal suspended them. He was going to give them in-school suspension, but they smell so bad, they aren't allowed back in school for a week."

"My parents are really angry. Marvin's grounded. He's not allowed to go anywhere except school and church. In fact, he has to sleep out in a tent in our backyard until he stops smelling like skunk. The only time he's allowed in the house is to go to the bathroom and to take tomato-juice baths."

I giggle. "Why tomato juice?"

"It helps get rid of skunk smell," Brandi says. "Now for Bulletin Number Four."

"Wow. It was a big news weekend," Naomi says.

I think about what a big news weekend it was for me, but I know that Brandi won't blab all of the stuff I told her when I went over to her house on Sunday.

"Number Four is about Mrs. Owen, the kindergarten teacher. She told my mother that this week she's going to have a new rule in class. During story hour, when the kids in her class are sitting on the floor listening, they are not allowed to touch her legs and tell her that she needs a shave."

Everyone laughs.

"I bet Mrs. Holt wouldn't let us do that either," Jimmy says.

Tiffani punches him on the arm. "You

are soooooooooo gross. Mrs. Owen has the little kids. They do stuff like that."

Tiffani should know. Her little brother is in that class.

"Most of us are more mature." She makes a face at Jimmy. "Of course, you just might be the exception."

I look at some of the kindergarteners, who are going down the slide.

Just last week, I saw Jimmy go down that same slide.

Actually, it was right before I went down that same slide.

"Bulletin Number Five." Brandi looks at me.

For a minute, I am very nervous. What if Brandi tells everyone about how my dad is going to move back and how much that upset my mom? What if she tells everyone how my mom called my dad up and they talked for a while and then my mom hung up on my dad? And how then my dad called up and when my mom answered, he hung up on her?

I definitely hope that my family is not part of the Brandi Bulletin Show.

"The last bulletin is about the sighting of Mr. Cohen . . . . . and Ms. Levine on Saturday night at the Multi-Plex, sharing a box of popcorn."

"OoOoOoOoOoOoOoOo," everyone says.

Bobby makes kissing sounds on his hand.

The bell rings.

It's time for school to begin.

I, Amber Brown, am glad that the weekend is over and, at least at school, it's back to normal.

I wonder what it's going to be like when my dad returns.

Chapter
Ten

Entering the classroom, I see that there is an extra desk.

I wonder what the new boy is going to be like.

Staring at the empty desk, I feel really weird.

It's not that I don't want new people in my class. . . . It's just that I don't want new people in my class RIGHT NOW.

"Class," Mrs. Holt says, "in about ten minutes, your new classmate will arrive. I want you to make him feel welcome."

Brandi raises her hand. "Mrs. Holt, what can you tell us about our new classmate?"

Looking up from her attendance book, Mrs. Holt stares at Brandi. "Do you want this information to help him feel welcome or is it for your latest bulletin?"

"Bulletin. Bulletin. Bulletin," the class says all together.

Brandi smiles. "Both."

Mrs. Holt smiles too. "OK. His name is Hal Henry . . . and I repeat, please help him to feel welcome. I know that you all will."

Brandi raises her hand. "May I please be Hal's special guide? I know how hard it is to be the new kid in school."

"Oooh!!!!!! You're a girl. You can't be his guide." Bobby Clifford crosses his eyes.

"Boys and girls can be friends," I say, thinking of Justin.

Then I think of Bobby and add, "Well, not always."

Then I think about Justin and wonder if he had a guide when he went to his new school.

There's a knock on our classroom door.

It's the vice principal with the new kid.

We all look at him.

He's got brown hair, brown eyes.

He looks at all of us.

He's also got ears that wiggle and eyes that cross.

"Hal," the vice principal says.

Hal's ears stop wiggling and his eyes stop crossing.

He's got a great smile.

"Welcome, Hal." Mrs. Holt smiles back at him and points to the empty seat.

Hal sits down.

Mrs. Holt says, "Brandi Colwin will be your guide if you have any questions."

"I'll be glad to help too," Bobby yells out. "I can wiggle my ears and cross my eyes too."

Bobby and Hal cross their eyes and wiggle their ears at each other.

Soon everyone in class is trying it, everyone except for Hannah Burton and the grown-ups.

Hal is definitely going to be an interesting addition to our class.

I bet Brandi is going to have fun being his guide. . . . She just better not like him more than she likes me.

I wonder if I, Amber Brown, can have a guide to help me through all of the changes in my life.

Chapter Eleven

"These are the best, the best, the very best bowling shirts ever." I hold one of them up.

My mom and Max look at each other and grin.

They helped the team design them.

We've already had one meeting, one practice.

I, Amber Brown, am team captain of "The Pinsters"—the "Head Pin." Brandi is on my team. So is the new kid, Hal, who says that he can wiggle his ears and cross his eyes while he bowls. The other two on the team are Tiffani Shroeder and Gregory Gifford.

Hannah Burton said that the only reason I'm team captain is because my stepfather is the coach.

I told her that the team voted for ME . . . . . and Max is not my stepfather, not yet. (Even though I really like Max, I'm not ready for the "step" step yet.)

"The shirts look soooo good."

They're white T-shirts, outlined in black so that they look like real bowling shirts, with our names printed over make-believe pockets. The back looks really great with the team name and the picture.

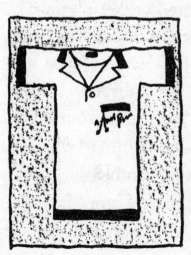

"Try it on," my mom says.

I go into the downstairs bathroom, take off my other T-shirt, and put the team shirt on.

Looking at myself in the mirror, I check out the front and then the back of the shirt.

It makes me feel like I will bowl even better when I wear it, maybe even break a hundred. (The highest score I've ever gotten was ninety-seven and that was with those "cheater" thingies in the gutter, so I couldn't get a gutter ball.)

I, Amber Brown, want "The Pinsters" to be the best team in the Pee-Wee league.

I, Amber Brown, want to understand why the league is called "Pee-Wee." Maybe because I'm standing in the bathroom, I think it's a weird name . . . but it does sound like something to do in a bathroom. Maybe the Pee-Wee Championship should be called the Toilet Bowl.

Going back down to the living room, I model the shirt for Mom and Max.

The phone rings.

My mom rushes to answer it.

She thinks I don't realize that ever since I got to the phone and talked to my father first, she now tries to answer the phone before me. If it's my dad, she goes into another room and talks to him and then she lets me talk to him.

She says she does that so that there will be no more misunderstandings.

She takes the portable phone into another room.

Max and I look at each other.

I sit down at the table and put my head on the table.

He pats my head.

It makes me feel a little like a dog, but it also makes me feel good because I know that Max is trying to make me feel better.

My mother walks back into the room and hands me the phone. "It's your father."

My father's first words to me are, "What is SHE saying about me?"

I decide to ignore that question and say, "Hi, Dad. Do you miss me? When are we going to see each other? Do you know yet?"

He smiles.

I can't see him on the telephone, but I can tell from his voice that he's smiling. "I'll be back for a visit next week. While

I'm there, I'll be meeting with my new bosses . . . and looking for an apartment. Amber, I want you to go with me when I look at apartments since it's also going to be your place. Then we'll go shopping and buy all new furniture for your room."

I don't know why I don't feel more excited, why there is a knot in my stomach. Actually, there's more than a knot. It's more like a giant knotted string ball in my stomach.

I, Amber Brown, am always begging to redo my room at home and my mom is always saying that I can't right now.

Now I have a chance to have a whole brand-new room and I'm feeling weird about it.

My father continues. "We'll get a television for your room and your own phone line and your own computer."

I think about how I'm always begging my mom to redo my room and how she's always saying, "Not now. Money's tight and we don't know how much longer we'll be living in this place, especially after the wedding."

My father is still talking. "We can get you bunk beds or one of those sneaker beds you've always wanted. Am I leaving anything out? Is there anything else that you want?"

I say, "Yes. I want you and Mom to stop fighting with each other."

I, Amber Brown, have given up wanting them to get back together. I just want the fighting to stop.

There's silence for a minute, and then my father says, "I can't wait to see you. When I get back, we'll go apartment hunting over the weekend."

"Just so it's not on Saturday afternoon when the bowling team is competing," I tell him.

"OK," he says. "I'll go to the game to watch my little girl bowl and then we'll search for an apartment and go shopping."

He's going to go to the game, the game that Max will be coaching . . . . the game that my mother will be cheering at.

My stomach really hurts.

Something tells me that it won't be just the bowling team that will be competing.

When I get off the phone with my dad, my mom asks, "What did HE say?"

I tell her about the apartment hunting

and how I'm going to get a room of my own and all new things.

My mom is quiet for a minute and then she says, "Maybe it's time to redo your room."

I, Amber Brown, have been waiting so long for her to say that, but I am beginning to think that it's not rooms that need to be done or redone. . . . It's the way that my parents are acting.

When my parents separated, I thought it couldn't get worse.

When they got divorced, I thought it couldn't get worse.

Now I'm getting worried.

I can't even begin to imagine how much worse it's going to get.

Chapter Twelve

I reread my dad's latest letter for the eighty-zillionth time.

The last line is "Things will be perfect when I come back and my little girl and I can make up for lost time."

How can we make up for lost time? I'm not the same little girl that I was when he left.

What can I do to make it "perfect"?

It's so hard.

If it's "perfect" for my dad, I know that it won't be "perfect" for my mom.

And what about me, Amber Brown?

How can it be "perfect" for me?

I was such a little kid when I thought what would be "perfect" would be my parents getting back together.

When I went to England over the summer, I still thought that maybe they would get back together.

I can't believe that was only a few months ago.

Everything feels so different.

I pick up my gorilla.

"Gorilla," I say, "before the divorce, my parents fought. Then when Dad moved to Paris, they didn't have anything to do with each other . . . . so no fighting. . . . At least not until I was supposed to visit my dad in Paris. . . . Then there was some trouble. . . . Now that Dad is coming back, the fighting has started again . . . and they act like I'm a little kid . . . that I'll just go along with what each of them wants. . . . How can I do that? They both want different things."

The gorilla, as always, says nothing.

I continue. "It's terrible. When they got divorced, they worked out who got what. . . . I'm the only thing that they couldn't give to just one of them . . . and now that Dad's moving back . . . they want to split me. . . . They call it shared custody, but I feel split."

The hairy ape still says nothing.

I get mad at him. "You don't understand. There's only one of you. What am I going to do when I go to Dad's and I need to talk to you and you're here? I can't carry you back and forth, take you to school with me. It would look really dumb for me, a fourth grader, to take a dumb stuffed animal to school."

I continue. "What am I supposed to do? Sometimes I feel like I'm the grown-up, the one who has to take care of both of them. Sometimes they want me to be so grown up . . . . and then I'm supposed to be their little girl. . . . . Each of their little girl. . . . You just don't understand, you ape. . . . I'm their little girl. . . . You're a little gorilla. . . . You're never going to have to change . . . . but I do have to change . . . because of my growth spurt . . . because my parents are spurting . . . or exploding, or something."

I feel so mad.

I throw the gorilla across the room.

"I'm sorry." I pick him up. "It's not your fault, I know."

Putting him on my dresser, I look at myself in the mirror.

I can see more of myself in the mirror.

Either the dresser is shrinking or I've gotten taller.

I can look at myself clearly . . . and I don't like what I see.

My stupid ponytails look so baby.

How are my parents going to take me seriously if I look like a little kid?

I rush downstairs.

"I hate my hair. I hate my hair. I hate my hair. I hate my hair. I hate my hair. I hate my hair. I hate my hair. I hate my hair. I hate my hair." Walking into the kitchen, I stand in front of my mother, who is making breakfast.

"Let me guess," she says, putting bacon into the pan. "You hate your hair."

I nod. "I hate my hair."

"Now, correct me if I'm wrong. You don't like your hair."

"Mom. Stop joking. I'm serious. I hate my hair." I hold it up on either side of my head. "This way I look like a horse with tails on each side of my face."

"It looks cute." My mom smiles. "I've always thought it's looked cute like that. You've been wearing your hair that way since you were little."

"Exactly," I say. "Since I was little. . . . . But now I'm in fourth grade and no one wears her hair like this anymore."

"It's so cute," she repeats.

"And look at this." I let my hair down. "I have split ends and the bangs are covering my eyes. I'm having a bad hair day. . . . . No, actually I'm having a bad hair life."

"Let me guess. You want to do something different with your hair." She starts making an omelette.

I nod.

My bangs cover my eyes.

She sighs. "I love the ponytails."

"Mom. I'm in the fourth grade . . . . remember?! Nobody wears her hair like this anymore . . . and even if they did, I don't want to anymore." I put a piece of bacon into my mouth.

She sighs. "You're growing up so fast."

I, Amber Brown, hope she remembers that when she and my dad make decisions about my life. I hope that she realizes that it's my hair, it's my life . . . and I have a say in what happens.

She sighs again. "OK. After breakfast, I'll call the salon and see if they can fit you in. While I get my hair trimmed and colored, maybe you can get a haircut."

"I'd like to get more than 'a hair' cut. . . . I'd like to get all of them cut." I grin at her.

She puts our breakfast on plates, we eat, and then we head off to the salon.

I'm ready.

Walking into the salon, I look around and try to figure out what I want to do with my hair.

Do I want them to trim it, just at the edges, to get rid of the split ends?

Do I want them to cut it shoulder length so that I can still put it up with ponytails and still be able to use scrunchies?

I, Amber Brown, don't know.

I just know that I want to get my hair cut.

I sit down in the waiting area.

My mom and I look at fashion magazines and try to pick out a haircut.

She points to one picture. "How about that look?"

Shaking my head, I make a face. "No. No. No. I'll look like an eggshell with bird poop on it."

"No you won't." My mom playfully taps my arm with the magazine. "You'll look cute."

Cute.

A woman comes up and takes me over to the sink to wash my hair.

Torture. It's total torture.

I've got to sit in this big uncomfortable chair with my head leaning back in this groove.

The hair washer must have learned how to shampoo at the School of Hair Pain.

"Stop squirming," she tells me.

Stop killing my head, I think, but I'm afraid to say it out loud in case she scrubs my head even harder.

Finally, I'm shampooed, cream-rinsed, and let free.

Even though there is a towel around my hurting neck, the water is dripping down

my back. It's dripping all the way down. It's making my underpants wet.

Sitting in the styling area, I wait for the haircut guy to come over.

I, Amber Brown, am getting very nervous.

He, my mom, and I talk about what to do.

I just want my hair to look wonderful. I want to look like I can handle anything and should be listened to.

"Trust me," he says, starting to cut.

Halfway through the cut, I realize that he
is cutting it too short.

"Stop!" I yell.

It's too late.

Chapter
Thirteen

I hate my hair. I hate my hair. I hate my hair. I hate my hair. I hate my hair. I hate my hair. I hate my hair. I hate my hair. I hate my hair.

I, Amber Brown, hate my hair.

I make one of my first grown-up decisions and it's a disaster.

I wonder if the rest of my life is going to be like this, if I can ever trust myself again.

The haircutting guy, who I now refer to as Hack, ruined my hair.

He cut it so that the rest of my hair is even with my ears. . . . . My bangs don't

even touch my eyebrows. And my eyebrows are going to catch cold.

When I want to chew on a strand of my hair, it doesn't even come close to my mouth.

I've had to change from hair chewing to nail chewing.

I'm running out of fingernails . . . and I don't think that I'm going to change to toenail biting.

I, Amber Brown, am never going to come out of my room.

When I go back to school, it's going to be awful.

The boys are going to tease me.

The new boy, Hal, already has given me a new nickname . . . . . " 'AMBERger Brown." I tried to explain that it was hambUrger, not hambErger, but he said, "Same difference." When he sees me now, I just know that he's going to call me "chopped 'Amberger."

There's a knock on the door.

"Go away," I say. "Nobody's here."

My mom knocks again.

I say nothing.

She walks in. "Amber. The mail has just arrived. There's a present for you from Aunt Pam."

"Bring it in here," I say.

She shakes her head. "No. If you want it, you're going to have to come downstairs and get it."

"Bring it up here," I say. "I am never leaving my room again."

"Amber Marie Brown." She's using that "I'm serious, you better stop this right now" voice. "Either you come down right now and look at it, or I'm putting it away for a while."

It's not fair. It's a present for me.

And anyway, I'm not sure that I believe that there really is a present for me. It's probably a trick.

I think about it.

My mom doesn't lie.

Aunt Pam does send me lots of surprises.

I go downstairs.

There is a package with a California postmark.

I open it . . . . . two wrapped presents, with an envelope.

I open the envelope first.

Aunt Pam and Mom have trained me to read the card before opening the present.

The front of the card is actually a picture that someone took of Aunt Pam and me in front of Big Ben in London.

Aunt Pam has drawn a speech balloon coming out of the clock. It's as if the clock is saying, "IT'S TIME TO GIVE AMBER BROWN AN 'I LOVE YOU' PRESENT."

Inside it says,

I saw these and thought of you....
...You know that you can call and
talk to me whenever you want to.
            Love,
            Aunt Pam

I open the first package.

It's personalized crayons with my name on them.

Aunt Pam knows how the kids are always saying, "Amber Brown is a crayon," and I'm always saying, "Amber Brown is not a crayon."

I can't believe that she found them.

It makes me laugh but I hope that none of the kids see them. I'll really get teased.

The next package is much bigger.

I unwrap it.

"Uggh," my mother says, "that's so gross."

I really laugh.

It is gross, so gross, so very gross.

It's a game called Gooey Louie.

I set it up.

It's a giant plastic head.

I put the "gooeys," green fluorescent snots, into Louie's nose, set up his brain, and get ready to play the game with my mom.

We keep putting our fingers up Louie's nose and pulling gooeys out of it.

There's one gooey that's secretly attached to something so that when that one gets pulled, Louie's brain pops out of the top of his head.

I really wish that Justin were here. He would love, Love, LOVE this game. Where he lives now in Alabama, he and his new friends have started a group called the Royal Order of the Snots. He even gave me something called Snap Snots, which you stick up your nose.

I am having such a good time, I've almost forgotten how upset I was.

Putting my hand on my hair, I remember why I was so upset.

My hair . . . .

I hate my hair.

"I hate my hair," I tell my mom. "It's all your fault that this happened."

She looks at me. "Why is it my fault? I liked it the way it looked. I told you not to cut it. . . . And anyway, your hair looks terrific with this style."

I pull out a gooey. "I hate my hair. It's all your fault . . . your fault and Dad's fault . . . I wouldn't have cut my hair if I didn't have to be more grown up, if you two would just stop fighting and just let ME be the child."

My mother pulls out a gooey and Louie's brain flies out.

She loses.

While I refill Louie's nose, I say, "I am really angry at you."

I say something that I once heard her say. "I'm so angry that I'm seeing red."

My mother looks serious for a minute and then she laughs.

"This is not funny." I slam Louie's nose down.

"I'm sorry," she says. "I just thought 'Amber Brown sees red.' That's very colorful."

My own mother, my own mother who named me, making fun of my name. . . . . It's just more than I can handle.

I try to stay angry, but I do think it's funny, kind of.

I put a gooey by her nose and say, "Careful . . . or I'm going to pull this and pop your brain out."

"You are so gross," my mom says.

"Thank you," I say.

My mom looks at me and gets serious. "Honey, are you really upset by what's happening?"

I nod.

Usually my mom is pretty smart about things. How can she not think all of this fighting bothers me?

"I hate it. I hate that you and Daddy got divorced. I hate that you don't want him to come back to this country. I hate that you two can't get along. I hate that you always call him HIM or HE and that he always calls you HER or SHE."

"It could be worse. We could be calling each other worse names." My mom tries to joke. "Like IT or WHAT'S-HIS- or -HER-FACE."

I don't say anything.

My mom makes me really mad when she tries to kid about something this serious . . . . when I'm trying to tell her something this important.

I, Amber Brown, am not just seeing red . . . . I'm seeing purple . . . . orange . . . . . magenta.

It's very quiet. I'm not saying anything. My mom is not saying anything. Gooey Louie is not saying anything.

My mom folds her arms in front of her and rests her head on them.

Finally, she raises her head and sighs. "I try so hard to be a good mother."

"I know," I say.

Even though I'm mad at her, I know that she tries hard, that she is a good mother.

"I'll call your dad and talk to him. I'll do my best. I hope that he'll do his best. If we need to, we'll get counseling," she says.

"Thanks." I get up and hug her.

She hugs me back.

We sit down and play Gooey Louie again.

Again, my mom makes his brain fly.

I, Amber Brown, am getting very good at this game.

I think about how Mr. Cohen, my third grade teacher, used to say, "Let your imagination soar."

He should see Louie.

Chapter Fourteen

"Hair today. Gone tomorrow." Hannah Burton looks up at me while we're choosing our bowling balls. "You looked better when your hair was covering your face."

I think about how I'm finally getting used to my hair, how in the beginning I wore my baseball cap to hide it.

It's been over a week and everyone else leaves me alone about my hair, but not Hannah.

I think about dropping the bowling ball on her foot but decide against it.

I hope that she drops a bowling ball on her own foot.

"Practice time," Max calls out. "Pinsters in Lane Six."

We rush over to our lanes.

The practice begins.

I have trouble concentrating.

My dad was supposed to meet me this morning before practice but his plane is late.

Now my mom is waiting at the house to talk to him about stuff, and then they're going to come over to the bowling alley together. I know that they've been talking to each other a lot on the phone.

It's hard to concentrate but I try to pay attention to what our team is doing.

It's Brandi's turn.

She starts walking down the lane with a bowling ball and then walks back. She picks up a second ball and throws them both down the alley at the same time.

Nine pins are knocked down.

One of the guys who works at the bowling alley comes over and yells at her.

Max goes over and calms the guy down. When the guy leaves, Max turns to Brandi and says, "Bulletin. Bulletin. Bulletin. . . . Late-breaking news. Brandi Colwin, future newscaster, is going to promise NEVER to do that again . . . or the next news flash will be that Ms. Colwin has been benched."

"I've never heard of a bowler getting benched," Hal says. "Wow, Brandi. That's cool."

She grins at him.

That makes me a little jealous and nervous but not a lot because Brandi has said that I'm still her best girl friend.

Max says, "Brandi."

Brandi tries to look sorry so that she doesn't get benched but I can tell that she had fun throwing the two balls down the lane at once.

"Max," Brandi says, "I promise to be good. Please, don't bench me."

"OK." Max tries to look very serious but I can tell that he's not too upset.

I, Amber Brown, would like to try throwing two balls down the alley, but it would be hard to do because Max is the coach.

Max is a great coach. He helps. He's fun. He's not too strict, but he's strict enough.

I'd be having a great time if I wasn't so worried about what's going to happen when my dad gets here.

"Your turn," Greg yells.

I pretend that the pins are everyone who is driving me nuts.

Strike.

I knock them all down.

Going back to my seat, I look around.

My parents are not here yet.

In Lane Ten, I see Hannah Burton start to bowl.

Miss. Miss. Miss, I think.

Hannah gets a gutter ball.

Yes.

Maybe my brain can will things to happen.

Hannah bowls again.

Miss. Miss. Miss, I think.

Hannah knocks them all down.

So much for my brain wishpower.

"Amber." I hear my father's voice.

I turn around.

My father is standing next to my mother.

"Daddy," I yell, not caring who hears me calling him Daddy.

I rush up to him, jump up, hug him, and wrap my legs around his waist, just like I did when I was little.

He holds me just like he did when I was little but I can feel his legs wobble just a bit.

"You got taller," he says.

I get down.

"And older," he says.

"So did you," I tease.

"Taller and older?" he teases back, standing up very straight.

I look at my dad.

He doesn't look as tall as he used to look.

"And balder," I tease him again.

I always used to tease him about his losing his hair and starting to look like my grandpa.

My dad pats the top of his head and then he looks over at my mom, who is standing next to Max, who has his arm around her waist.

Max has a lot of hair.

My dad looks back at me. His eyes are a little sad.

"I love the way you look, Daddy," I say, hugging him again.

"I've missed you so much," my dad says softly. "I was wrong to let them transfer me so far away. I need to be closer to my little girl. . . . It got so lonely there."

It makes me feel so good to know that he felt lonely without me.

Then, for a second, I think about how he didn't always stay in touch, how he told me about this woman he was dating and about her kid. So he wasn't always so lonely.

But then I stop thinking about that.

My dad is back . . . and he loves me.

"Your turn, Amber," Greg yells.

Greg bowls after me and he hates to wait.

I think Greg would like it best if he could be his own bowling team and never wait for anyone else to take a turn.

I hug my father again and then I go back to the alley.

Before bowling, I turn around.

Max and Mom are standing there, together. Their arms are around each other's
waists.

There's a look that my mom gets on her
face when she's a little nervous. She's got it
now.

I look at my father, who is standing there
alone.

"Go!" Gregory yells.

I turn back to the alley.

It's hard to keep my mind on the game

when so much is going on in my real life.

My life is a little like my bowling.

There's always something new to learn, some way to do better.

It's just about impossible to be perfect all the time. In fact, some days it's hard to do anything right. But sometimes things go really well. There are a lot of new things to learn, a lot of new rules and regulations.

Things don't always work out the way I want them to.

But I'm learning.

I'm learning to be part of a team, even if the team doesn't always do what I want.

I'm also learning to be the best that I can be on my own.

I may never bowl a perfect game.

I may never have a perfect life.

There is one thing, though, that I know for sure.

I, Amber Brown, am going to be a winner.

Turn the page
for a preview of

AMBER BROWN
IS FEELING BLUE

Chapter One

"Ta-da, dinner is served." Brenda, my Amber-sitter, comes into the living room. This week her hair is lime green and spiky.

I am lying down on the floor, doing my homework.

Brenda claps her hands. "Tonight I have made an amazing meal. I call it 'Mischief Night Delight.'"

If she thinks that this meal is amazing, that makes me more than a little nervous. Brenda thought it was perfectly normal when she made "Tuna Fish Delish." That had little chunks of celery and marshmallows in it.

I look up at Brenda.

She's wearing shocking-pink tights with a huge T-shirt, one that says PLAYS WELL WITH OTHERS. Mom and I gave it to her for her birthday last month.

I, Amber Brown, picked out the T-shirt.

I'm wearing the one my mom bought for me to wear when Brenda comes over to Amber-sit. Mine says NEEDS SUPERVISION.

Sometimes my mom thinks that she's very funny.

I get up, and we go into the kitchen.

Brenda has the table all set. "It's the Mischief Night menu."

I look at the table. In the center, there is chili made with ground meat. In the middle of the meat, on top, she has placed two gumballs, which look like eyes.

Avocado halves are filled with green Jell-O.

She's even used the plastic pumpkin that my mom will fill tomorrow with the candy

2

that we're giving out for Halloween. It's filled with cauliflower.

"It looks like the pumpkin's brains. Isn't that cool?" Brenda looks pleased with herself.

The cauliflower is steaming and looks very squishy, and there's tomato sauce poured over it to look like blood.

"Yum," Brenda says.

I just look at it.

"Yum," Brenda repeats.

Brenda pretends to be the waiter and pulls out my chair.

I sit down.

She pretends to read from a menu, even though it is actually a serving spoon. "What would you like to order from our liquid list? Our milk is a very good year."

I laugh.

Whenever I see someone in a movie ordering wine, the waiter always says things like "This is a very good year."

Somehow I don't think old milk would be too delicious.

"Actually, the milk is a very good *week* . . . this one," Brenda says.

"Fine." I look at the meal. "Then I will have a glass of milk. Which milk, do you think, goes better with this food? Chocolate? Vanilla?"

"Might I suggest the strawberry? It would look good with the orange of the pumpkin, the brown of the meat, the red of the pumpkin blood," Brenda says, going over to the blender and putting in some milk and some strawberries.

We sit down to eat.

I stare at the meal but don't eat anything.

"It won't kill you. I promise." Brenda starts eating. "Yum."

Brenda said "Yum" the time she ate the tuna-and-marshmallow meal. THAT was definitely not a "Yum" meal.

I take a tiny taste of each thing.

It is an amazing meal. What is amazing is that it tastes good.

"So, what are you going to wear tomorrow for Halloween?" I ask.

Brenda smiles. "For Halloween, I'm going to dress 'normal.' I'm going to wear a wig that is a normal color and has a normal boring cut. And I'm going to wear one of my mother's normal dresses and a pair of heels. That will be my costume."

I tell her what I'm going to wear even though I'm keeping it a secret from everyone else. No one else will know until tomorrow.

"So," she says, changing the subject, "when is your dad moving back here from Paris?

"In just two weeks." I clap my hands. "I can't wait."

Brenda grins at me. "You are so excited. Tell me about your dad." Because Brenda became my Amber-sitter after my parents divorced, after my dad moved to Paris, she's never met him.

I describe my dad. "He's not real skinny. He's not real fat. . . . He's got a real nice smile when he's happy. . . . Sometimes he tells very corny jokes. . . . He's losing his hair . . . only when I tell him that, he says that it's not lost, that it's just flown off in a hairplane."

Brenda smiles. "He sounds funny."

I nod. "He is . . . or, he was. I've only seen him twice since he moved to Paris . . . once in England . . . and a couple of weeks ago, when he came back to see about his new job . . . and to see ME. But we talk on the phone all the time, and he says that when he moves back, he's going to spend a lot of time with me . . . he's going to take me on trips, to the movies, to lots of places . . . and when he gets an apartment, it's going to have two bedrooms so that I will always have a place to stay with him. And I can pick out all new furniture and decorate it the way I want."

"Cool." Brenda takes a sip of her strawberry milk. "You're so lucky."

I look at Brenda and think about how she has no father because he was killed in a car crash almost a year ago, before I knew her.

She looks sad.

I reach over and pat her on her hand. "When Dad moves back, I'm going to ask him if you can do some stuff with us . . . not as my Amber-sitter, but as my friend."

Brenda puts her hand on top of mine. "If I had a sister, I'd want her to be just like you."

"Me too," I say. "If I had a sister, I'd want her to be just like you."

I pat her hand again and then stand up. "I've got to get something. I'll be right back."

Running up the stairs to my room, I open my closet door, and take a box off the top shelf.

I haven't shown it to anyone else yet. It's like it was my own little secret, my own little private special thing.

There's no way I can show it to my mom.

I don't think she's going to like it.

There's no way I can show it to Max, the guy my mom is going to marry.

I don't think he's going to like it either. I think he's gotten used to being the only grown-up guy in my everyday life.

Rushing down the steps with it, I put the box on the table, and open it up.

Inside is the "Countdown to Dad" book, which I got in the mail last week.

My dad made it for me.

It's made out of construction paper and has four pages.

The first is the cover. On it, he's written "Countdown to Dad" and drawn lots of hearts.

The other three pages are made up to look like a weekly calendar, with numbered squares. The numbers go from twenty-one to zero. In each square is a picture of Dad and me. There's also a tiny box where I can check off each day when it's over. The first

photo is of the day when he and Mom brought me home from the hospital when I was a baby. Mom took that picture (and most of the others). The rest of the pictures also show Dad and me together. As the countdown goes on, I get older and Dad gets balder. The next-to-last picture is labeled "One more day until I'm back and can hug my little girl." It's a picture that Aunt Pam took of my dad and me when we were in London. I have chicken-pox scabs on my face. The last picture is one that Brandi took of my dad and me at the bowling alley, when he was here to visit and work out moving back.

On the "Zero Square," he's written "Reunion" and he's drawn more hearts.

Only fourteen more days to check off. . . . I can't wait.

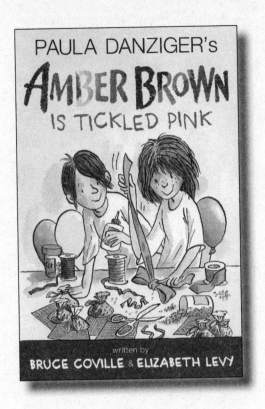

PAULA DANZIGER's
AMBER BROWN
IS TICKLED PINK

written by
BRUCE COVILLE & **ELIZABETH LEVY**

Amber can't wait to be Best Child when her mom and Max get married, but planning a wedding comes with lots of headaches. Amber can't find the right dress, her dad keeps making mean cracks about Max, and everyone is going crazy over how much things cost. Her mother even suggests they go to city hall and skip the party altogether!

Justin and his family are supposed to come for the wedding, and Amber has been looking forward to that for months. Adults sure can be a lot of work, but if Amber can make this wedding work, it will all be worth it.